The Boy Who Cried Wolf

ADAPTED BY
Teresa Mlawer

ILLUSTRATED BY
Olga Cuéllar

chosen spot
publishing

Once upon a time, there was a young shepherd boy named Peter. He lived with his parents in a village on a hillside.

Peter took care of the other villagers' sheep to make some money and help his parents.

Every day, Peter took the sheep to the hilltop.

From there, he could see all the houses in the village.

He always went with Lucas, his sheep dog, who helped him herd the sheep together.

Before Peter left the house to take care of the sheep, his mother prepared a basket with food. She also warned him to watch out for any wolves that might be on the prowl in search of sheep.

Looking after sheep was a boring job. Peter was always alone and he would often keep busy by counting sheep during the day or the stars at night.

One morning, when Lucas had gone off to chase some rabbits,
Peter got so bored he decided to play a trick on the villagers.

He climbed to the top of the hill and started shouting in the direction of the village, "Wolf! Wolf! The wolf is coming!"

The villagers were busy working in the town's vegetable garden when they heard the boy's cries.

They immediately ran towards the hill, armed with their farming tools, to chase the wolf and save their herd.

When the villagers reached the top of the hill, they saw that the sheep were grazing peacefully, and Peter was nowhere to be found.

Fearing the worst, the villagers began to search for the boy. "Peter! Peter! Where are you?" they shouted.

Finally, his mother spotted him hiding behind a rock, roaring with laughter.

"Peter, your irresponsible behavior has given us all a terrible fright," his mother said. "You must apologize to everyone right away."

Peter felt very bad, so he looked at the villagers and said, "I'm truly sorry. I will never do it again."

For a few days, Peter kept his word, but one afternoon he began to feel lonely and bored again.

Forgetting his promise, he raced to the top of the hill and again started shouting, "Wolf! Wolf! The wolf is coming!"

This time, many of the villagers paid no attention to Peter's cries for help. They thought he was playing another one of his tricks. However, his parents and a few other people ran

to the top of the hill to help Peter, but when they arrived they found him laughing hysterically.

The villagers were very angry with Peter. They warned him they would not come if he cried wolf again.

After realizing how foolishly he acted, Peter promised himself he would not play any more tricks that would upset his parents and the villagers.

Peter continued to take the sheep to the hilltop every day.
He kept himself busy by playing with Lucas or reading a book.

Then one evening, as he was resting under a tree,
he heard a noise. When he looked down he saw two red
lights glowing at him from the nearby bushes.

Peter quickly realized he was looking into the eyes of a fierce wolf that was staring at his sheep. He jumped to his feet, ran to the edge of the hill and cried out, "Wooolf! Wooolf! The wolf is here! He's taking the sheep!"

The villagers heard his cries, but not a single one of them ran to help him.

Realizing that no one was going to come, Peter decided to take action and save the sheep himself.

He grabbed his food basket and threw it with all his strength, hitting the wolf on the snout.

Frightened, the wolf ran off into the forest.

When he returned home that night, he told his parents
what had happened. Although they were shocked, they listened
to everything he had to say. When he finished they said,

"Peter, do you see what can happen when people don't tell the truth? We hope that you've finally learned your lesson. Still, we are very proud of you for being brave and saving the sheep all by yourself."

What lesson have we learned from his fable?

It's important to always tell the truth. Nobody believes people who lie, even when they are telling the truth.

FOR INFORMATION, PLEASE CONTACT CHOSEN SPOT PUBLISHING, P.O. BOX 266, CANANDAIGUA, NEW YORK, 14424

ISBN 978-0-9864313-7-1   10 9   PRINTED IN CHINA